TIMELESS

THE CALL
OF THE WILD

Jack London

– ADAPTED BY –

Stephen Feinstein

SADDLEBACK
EDUCATIONAL PUBLISHING

TIMELESS CLASSICS

Literature Set 1 (1719-1844)

A Christmas Carol
The Count of Monte Cristo
Frankenstein
Gulliver's Travels
The Hunchback of Notre Dame
The Last of the Mohicans

Oliver Twist
Pride and Prejudice
Robinson Crusoe
The Swiss Family Robinson
The Three Musketeers

Literature Set 2 (1845-1884)

The Adventures of Huckleberry Finn
The Adventures of Tom Sawyer
Around the World in 80 Days
Great Expectations
Jane Eyre
The Man in the Iron Mask

Moby Dick
The Prince and the Pauper
The Scarlet Letter
A Tale of Two Cities
20,000 Leagues Under the Sea

Literature Set 3 (1886-1908)

The Call of the Wild
Captains Courageous
Dracula
Dr. Jekyll and Mr. Hyde
The Hound of the Baskervilles
The Jungle Book

Kidnapped
The Red Badge of Courage
The Time Machine
Treasure Island
The War of the Worlds
White Fang

SADDLEBACK
EDUCATIONAL PUBLISHING
www.sdlback.com

ISBN-13: 978-1-61651-071-8
ISBN-10: 1-61651-071-4
eBook: 978-1-60291-805-4

Printed in the United States of America
15 14 13 12 11   1 2 3 4 5

| Contents |

| 1 |
Trouble Ahead

Buck did not read the newspapers. If he did, he would have seen some bad news. Trouble was coming. Not just for himself, but for every dog with strong muscles, from Puget Sound to San Diego. This was because, in the Arctic darkness, a precious yellow metal—gold—had been found.

Thousands of men were rushing to the frozen Northland. These men needed dogs. They wanted heavy dogs with strong muscles and furry coats. Big dogs would be able to work hard. And their furry coats would protect them from the cold.

Buck lived on a large estate in the sunny Santa Clara Valley. Judge Miller's place, it was called. The house stood back from the road. It was half-hidden among the trees. A wide porch ran around its four sides. At the rear of the house were stables, where a dozen grooms worked. There were rows of servants' cottages. And there were long grape arbors, green pastures, orchards, and berry patches. There was also a water pump for the well and for a big cement swimming tank. Judge Miller's sons took a dip in the tank every morning.

Buck ruled over this great estate. Here he was born. Here he had lived all four years of his life. There were other dogs here, but they did not count. They came and went. Many of them lived in the kennels. Some, such as Toots and Ysabel, lived in hidden corners of the house. On the other hand there were the fox terriers. These dogs would yelp at Toots and Ysabel looking out the windows at them.

But Buck was neither house dog nor kennel dog. The whole place was his. He went into the swimming tank or went hunting with the Judge's sons. He would go with Mollie and Alice, the Judge's daughters, on early morning walks. On winter nights he would lie at the Judge's feet by the fire in the library. He carried the Judge's grandsons on his back, or rolled them in the grass. He roamed wherever he pleased. For he was king over all the creeping, crawling, flying things of Judge Miller's place, humans included.

Buck's father was Elmo, a huge St. Bernard. Elmo had been the Judge's constant companion. It seemed that Buck was going to be very much like his father. Buck was smaller, though—he weighed only 140 pounds. His mother, Shep, had been a Scotch shepherd dog. Buck took great pride in himself and carried himself like a king. Hunting and other outdoor activity had kept down the fat and hardened his muscles.

This was the kind of dog Buck was in the fall of 1897. But because Buck did not read the newspapers, he did not know that gold had been discovered in the Klondike. And he did not know that one man at Judge Miller's place was about to change his life forever.

Manuel, one of the gardener's helpers, had a terrible weakness—he loved to gamble. And in order to gamble, he needed money. But the wages of a gardener's helper are barely enough to support a wife and children, let alone to gamble.

One night the Judge was at a meeting of the Raisin Growers' Association. His sons were busy planning a sports event. No one saw Manuel and Buck go off through the orchard. Buck thought they were just out for an evening walk. No one saw them arrive at the little train station known as College Park—nobody except the man who was waiting there for them. When this man talked with Manuel, money passed between them.

"You might wrap up the goods before you deliver them," the stranger said gruffly. Manuel doubled a piece of thick rope under the collar around Buck's neck.

"Twist it, and you'll choke him plenty," said Manuel. The stranger grunted in agreement.

Buck had accepted the rope with quiet dignity. He had learned to trust people he knew. He gave them credit for a wisdom beyond his own. But when the ends of the rope were placed in the stranger's hands, Buck growled. He did this to show the men he didn't like what was happening. His pride led him to think that this was all he needed to do. Once the men saw he wasn't happy, they would remove the rope.

But to Buck's surprise the rope tightened around his neck, shutting off his breath. In quick rage he sprang at the stranger, who was ready for him. The man grabbed him by the throat, and with a twist, threw Buck over on his back. Then the rope grew even tighter. Buck struggled in a fury, his tongue hanging out of his mouth, his big chest heaving. Never in his life had he been so badly treated! And never in his life had he been so *angry*. But as the rope tightened, his strength left him. Soon his eyes glazed over. He knew nothing when the train stopped and the two men threw him into the baggage car.

| 2 |

A Kidnapped King

The next thing Buck knew was that his tongue hurt. He was being jolted along in some kind of car. Then the loud shriek of the train whistle told him where he was. He had traveled too often with the Judge not to know the feeling of riding in a baggage car. He opened his eyes.

The stranger sitting beside him sprang for Buck's throat. But Buck was too quick for him. His jaws closed on the man's hand. And they didn't relax until Buck's senses were choked out of him once more.

"Yep, has fits," the stranger said, hiding his torn hand. He was speaking to the baggageman, who had heard the sounds of struggle. "I'm taking him up to San Francisco for the boss. A dog doctor there thinks he can cure him."

Later that night, the man told a bartender what had happened. By then he was in a little shed in back of a bar on the San Francisco waterfront.

"All I got is fifty for this job," the stranger said, "and I wouldn't do it again for a thousand, cold cash."

His hand was wrapped in a bloody cloth. The right leg of his pants was torn from knee to ankle.

"How much did the other man get?" the bartender asked.

"A hundred," was the reply. "He wouldn't take a penny less, so help me."

"That makes a hundred and fifty," the bartender said. "And he's worth it, for sure."

The kidnapper removed the bloody cloth and looked at his torn hand. "If I don't get rabies from this—"

"It'll be because you were born to hang," laughed the bartender. "Here, lend me a hand," he added.

Buck was dazed and suffering terrible pain in his throat. But now he tried to face the men. Half the life had been choked out of him. Yet again and again he was thrown down and choked. Finally the men were able to file the heavy brass collar from his neck. Then the rope was removed, and Buck was flung into a crate that was like a cage.

There he lay for the rest of the night, nursing his anger and wounded pride. Buck could not understand what it all meant. What did they want with him, these strange men? Why were they keeping him locked up in this narrow crate? He did not know why. But he had the feeling that something terrible was going to happen to him.

Several times during the night he sprang to his feet when the shed door rattled open. He was expecting to see the Judge, or the boys at least. But each time it was the ugly face of the bartender looking in at him by the light of a candle. And each time the happy bark that had welled up in Buck's throat was twisted into a growl.

Soon the bartender left him alone. In the morning, four men came and picked up the crate. This meant more trouble, Buck decided, for the men were evil-looking.

When Buck raged at them through the bars, they laughed and poked sticks at him. At first Buck attacked the sticks with his teeth. Then he saw that this was what the men wanted. So he lay down silently and allowed the crate to be lifted into a wagon.

Then Buck, in his crate, began a passage through many hands. Clerks in the express office took charge of him. Then he was put in another wagon. Next, a truck carried him, along with many other boxes, onto a ferry boat. After he was moved off the ferry into a railroad station, he was finally put in an express railroad car.

For two days and nights in the express car, Buck neither ate nor drank. When the express men tried to come near him, he growled at them. The men got back at Buck by teasing him. When Buck flung himself against the bars, they laughed at him and continued to tease him. They growled and barked like mad dogs, flapping their arms and crowing. Buck knew this was all very silly. But for this reason it was all the more outrage to his dignity.

Buck's anger grew and grew. He did not mind the hunger so much. But the lack of water caused him great suffering. In fact, the ill treatment had given him a fever.

Buck was glad for one thing, though. The rope was off his neck. That had given the men the upper hand. But now that it was off, he would show them. They would *never* get another rope around his neck. His mind was made up about that.

During his two days and nights in the express car, Buck had turned into a raging beast. His large eyes had become red and menacing. So changed was Buck that the Judge himself would not have recognized him. The express men breathed easier when they put him off the train at Seattle.

Four men carefully carried the crate from the wagon into a small back yard. There were high walls around the yard. A big man wearing a red sweater came out and signed the order for the driver. That man, Buck knew, would be the next one to mistreat him. Buck threw himself at the bars. The man smiled grimly, and brought out a hatchet and a club.

"You ain't going to take him out now?" the driver asked.

"Sure," the man said, driving the hatchet into one end of the crate.

The four men who had carried in the crate quickly scattered. From safe spots on top of the wall, they got ready to watch the show.

Buck rushed at the splintering wood, sinking his teeth into it. Wherever the hatchet fell on the outside, he was there on the inside, snarling and growling. Buck was as eager to get out as the man in the red sweater was to get him out.

"Now, you red-eyed devil," the man said.

He had made an opening big enough for Buck's body to fit through. At the same time he dropped the hatchet and shifted the club to his right hand.

Buck truly looked like a red-eyed devil as he readied himself to spring. His hair was bristling and his mouth foaming. There was a mad glitter in his bloodshot eyes. Straight at the man he threw his 140 pounds of fury, powered by the anger of two days and nights. But in midair, just as his jaws were about to close on the man, he got a shock. It stopped his body and snapped his jaw closed. He turned over, hitting the ground on his back and side.

Buck had never been struck by a club before—and he did not understand. With a snarl that was part bark and part scream, he leaped to his feet and then into the air. Again the shock came and brought him crashing to the ground. This time he was aware of the club, but he was too mad to stop. A dozen times he charged, and a dozen times the club broke the charge and smashed him down.

After one really strong blow, Buck crawled to his feet, too dazed to rush. He moved weakly about, blood flowing from his nose, mouth, and ears. His beautiful coat was splattered with spots of blood.

The man in the red sweater then gave him a frightful blow on the nose. All the pain Buck had felt up to now was nothing compared to this. With a roar almost like a lion's, he threw himself at the man. But the man, shifting the club from right to left, caught Buck under the jaw. The blow twisted Buck upward and backward. The big dog went through a complete circle in the air, and half of another. Finally he crashed to the ground on his head and chest.

For the last time Buck rushed. Then the man struck another mighty blow, and Buck went down for good.

Buck's senses slowly came back to him, but not his strength. For a long time he lay where he had fallen. From there he studied the man in the red sweater.

"Answers to the name of Buck," the man said to himself. He was reading from the bartender's letter, which described the crate and its contents. "Well, Buck, my boy," he said in a friendly voice, "we've had our little run-in. The best thing we can do now is to let it go at that. You've learned your place, and I know mine. Be a good dog and all will go well. Be a bad dog, and I'll knock the stuffing out of you. Understand?"

As he spoke, he patted the head he had so cruelly pounded. Although Buck's hair bristled at the touch of the man's hand, he didn't complain. When the man brought him water, he drank eagerly. Later, he ate a large meal of raw meat, chunk by chunk, from the man's hand.

Buck was beaten, he knew that. But he was not broken. He saw, once and for all, that he stood no chance against a man with a club. He had learned a lesson—one that he would not forget for the rest of his life. That club was Buck's introduction to the rule of primitive law, and he had met that law halfway. But the facts of life had taken on a meaner look. Buck was determined to face that look unafraid, and with all of his cunning.

As the days went by, more dogs arrived, in crates and at the ends of ropes. Some came quietly, and some came raging and roaring, just as he had come.

One and all, Buck watched them fall into

the hands of the man with the red sweater. Again and again, as he saw what happened to each dog, the lesson was driven home to Buck. *A man with a club was a lawgiver.* Yet, although man was a master to be obeyed, it was not necessary to cower before him. Of this Buck would never be guilty.

| 3 |

The Journey North

Now and again men came by to talk to the man in the red sweater. Whenever money passed between them, the strangers took one or more of the dogs away with them. Buck wondered where they went, for they never came back. All of this made Buck feel fearful about the future. He was glad each time he was not chosen.

Yet Buck's turn finally came. One day a scrawny little man came to see the man in the red sweater. The man spoke broken English and used many strange words which Buck could not understand.

"Sacredam!" the little man cried, when his eyes lit upon Buck. "That one bully dog, eh? How much?"

"Three hundred—and a present at that," replied the man in the red sweater.

Perrault grinned. The price of dogs had been shooting up because of the demand. He knew this was not an unfair sum for so fine an animal. The messages of the Canadian government would not travel slower because of this animal. Perrault knew dogs. When he looked at Buck, he recognized that this dog was one in a thousand. "Or maybe one in ten thousand," he said to himself.

Buck saw the scrawny man give money to the man in the red sweater. He was not surprised when he and Curly, a good-natured Newfoundland, were led away by the strange little man. That was the last Buck ever saw of the man in the red sweater.

Soon the two dogs were loaded on a ship. As Curly and Buck looked back at Seattle from the deck of the *Narwhal,* it was the last time they would see the warm Southland.

After Perrault took the dogs below, he turned them over to a giant called François. While Buck developed no love for these French-Canadians, he did grow to respect them. He quickly learned that Perrault and François were fair men. They were calm and evenhanded. And they were too wise in the way of dogs to be fooled by them.

Buck and Curly joined two other dogs on the *Narwhal*. One of them was a big, snow-white dog from Spitzbergen. He had been bought from a whaling captain. Spitz was friendly—in a sly sort of way. He would smile into one's face while thinking up some sneaky trick. For example, he stole from Buck's food at the first meal. As Buck sprang to punish him, the lash of François's whip sang through the air. The whip reached the white dog's back. There was nothing for Buck to do but to take back the bone. That was fair of the giant, Buck decided. His opinion of François improved.

The other dog showed no interest in the newcomers, nor did he try to steal from them. Dave was a gloomy beast. He quickly showed Curly that all he wanted was to be left alone. In fact, he made it clear that there would be trouble if he were *not* left alone. Beyond eating and sleeping, he took interest in nothing.

When the *Narwhal* crossed Queen Charlotte Sound, the ship rolled and bucked like a wild animal. Buck and Curly grew excited, half wild with fear. But Dave just raised his head and looked at them. Then he yawned and went to sleep again.

As the ship headed north, one day was very much like another. But it was clear to Buck that the weather was growing steadily colder. At last, one morning, the ship's propeller was quiet. Buck knew that a change was at hand.

François leashed the dogs and brought them on deck. At his first step upon the cold deck, Buck saw white stuff falling through the air. Sniffing it, he licked some up on his tongue. It bit like fire, and was gone in the next instant. This puzzled him. He tried it again, with the same result. The people around him laughed. Buck felt ashamed; he knew not why. For it was his first snow.

| 4 |

The Law of
Club and Fang

Buck's first day in the wild Northland was like a nightmare. Every hour was filled with shock and surprise. After all, he had been suddenly jerked from the heart of civilization and flung into the very heart of wildness.

The place was called Dyea Beach, and here there was neither peace, nor rest, nor a moment's safety. All was confusion and action. Every moment life and limb were in peril. One needed to be constantly alert, for these dogs and men were not town dogs and men. They were truly savages, all of them—creatures who knew no rule but the law of club and fang.

Buck had never seen dogs fight as these

wolfish creatures fought. He was soon to learn an unforgettable lesson. Curly, in her friendly way, had approached a husky dog the size of a wolf. With no warning, there had been a flash of teeth, and Curly's face was ripped open from eye to jaw.

It was the wolf manner of fighting—to strike and leap away. Thirty or forty huskies quickly surrounded the two fighting dogs, eagerly licking their chops. As Curly rushed at her attacker, he knocked her off her feet. This was what the other huskies were waiting for. They quickly closed in upon her, snarling and yelping. Curly was soon buried beneath them, screaming with agony.

Buck was shocked by the sudden attack. He saw François, swinging an axe, spring into the mess of dogs. Three men with clubs were helping him to scatter them. It did not take long. Curly lay in the bloody snow, limp and lifeless, torn almost to pieces.

That scene often came back to trouble Buck in his sleep. So that was the way it was. No fair play. Once down, that was the end of you. Well, he would see to it that he never went down. And when Curly went down, Buck saw Spitz run out his tongue in a way he had of laughing. From that moment on Buck hated him.

Now Buck received another shock. François fastened a harness on him, just as the grooms had harnessed the horses at home. Buck was put to work with the other dogs, pulling François on a sled. They went to the forest at the edge of the valley, and returned with a load of firewood. Though this work was all new and strange to Buck, he did his best.

François used a whip to make sure his dogs obeyed him. Spitz was the lead dog. He and Dave, by jerking and nipping at Buck, showed the new dog the proper way to pull a sled. Buck learned easily and made rapid progress. Before they returned to camp, he knew enough to stop at "ho," and to go ahead at "mush." He learned to swing wide on the bends. And he learned to keep clear of the wheeler when the loaded sled shot downhill at the dogs' heels.

"Three very good dogs," François told Perrault. "That Buck, him pull like all hell. I teach him quick as anything." By afternoon, Perrault returned with two more huskies, Billee and Joe. Billee was good natured, but Joe was always snarling. Buck greeted them in a friendly way, while Dave ignored them. Spitz attempted to show them who was boss.

By evening, Perrault brought along another dog—an old husky with a battle-scarred face and a single eye. He was called Sol-leks, which means Angry One. He asked nothing, gave nothing, expected nothing. Even Spitz left him alone. Buck made the mistake of approaching Sol-leks on his blind side. The old husky whirled upon Buck and slashed his shoulder to the bone.

That night Buck faced the great problem of sleeping. The tent, lit by a candle, glowed warmly in the midst of the white plain. But when Buck entered it, Perrault and François chased him back out into the cold. Buck lay down on the snow to sleep. But the frost soon drove him, shivering, to his feet. He wandered among the tents, but one place was as cold as another.

Finally he decided to see how his teammates were making out. But he couldn't find them—they had disappeared. He looked all over the camp, but there was no trace of them. As he circled the tent, the snow suddenly gave way beneath him. Buck sprang away, but when he heard a friendly little yelp, he went back to investigate. Curled up under the snow in a snug ball lay Billee.

Another lesson. So *that* was the way they did it! Buck picked a spot and dug a hole for himself in the snow. The heat from his body quickly filled the space and he fell into a sound sleep.

In the morning Buck was awakened by the noises of the camp. At first he did not know where he was. It had snowed during the night, and he was completely buried. With the snow pressing in on him on every side, a wave of fear swept through him. It was a wild thing's fear of the trap. With a loud snarl, Buck leaped out of the snow. When he saw the white camp spread out before him, he knew where he was. He remembered everything that had happened to him from the time he went for a walk with Manuel.

A shout from François greeted Buck. "See, what I say?" the dog-driver cried to Perrault. "That Buck for sure learn quick as anything."

Perrault nodded. Because his job was to carry important messages for the Canadian government, he was anxious to get the best dogs. And he was very pleased with Buck.

Three more huskies were added to the team, making a total of nine. Soon they were in harness and swinging up the trail toward the Dyea Canyon. Buck was glad to be moving. He was surprised by the eagerness of the whole team, and especially by the change in Dave and Sol-leks. They seemed like new dogs now, alert and active. It was as if the toil of the traces—the work of pulling the sled—was all that they lived for.

Dave was wheeler, the dog just in front of the sled. Pulling in front of him was Buck; then came Sol-leks. The rest of the team was strung out ahead, single file, to the leader. That position was filled by Spitz.

It was a hard day's run, up the Canyon, past the timberline, across glaciers and snowdrifts hundreds of feet deep, and over the great Chilcoot Divide. Late that night they pulled into the huge camp at Lake Bennett. There, thousands of gold-seekers were building boats to be ready for the breakup of ice in the spring.

That day they had made forty miles, the

trail being packed. But in the following days, they had to break their own trail. They had to work harder, and they made poorer time. While François rode on the sled, guiding it at the gee-pole, Perrault usually went ahead of the team. He packed the snow with webbed shoes to make it easier for them.

Day after day, Buck toiled at the traces. Always, they pitched camp after dark, eating their bit of fish and crawling to sleep in the snow. Buck was always hungry. He was given a pound and a half of salmon each day. But that was never enough to fill him, and he suffered constant hunger pangs.

Buck learned that unless he ate very quickly, his mates would steal part of his food. He also learned to take what did not belong to him—if he could get away with it. One day he saw Pike, one of the new dogs, steal a slice of bacon when Perrault's back was turned. The next day, Buck stole a whole chunk of bacon. Another dog, Dub, was punished for it.

This first theft showed that Buck could survive in the Northland, under the law of club and fang. It showed that he was able to adapt to changing conditions. Not being able to do so would have meant swift and terrible death. Buck learned to eat anything. His muscles became hard as iron. And his sense of sight, smell, and hearing became very sharp.

Not only did Buck learn by experience, but instincts long dead came alive again. Something inside him seemed to remember a time when wild dogs ran in packs through the ancient forests. On still, cold nights, he pointed his nose at a star and howled long and wolflike. It was as if, through him, his ancestors were howling down through the centuries.

| 5 |
Fight to the Death

The spirit of the wild beast became stronger in Buck. It grew and grew under the fierce conditions of trail life. Buck was too busy getting used to his new life to feel at ease. So not only did he not pick fights, but he avoided them whenever possible. And although he continued to feel bitter hatred toward Spitz, he kept his feelings to himself.

Spitz, however, must have felt that Buck was a dangerous rival. He never missed a chance to show his teeth. He even went out of his way to bully Buck. And he would always try to start a fight that could end only in the death of one or the other.

This might have taken place early in the trip had it not been for an unexpected event. At the end of this day they made camp on the shore of Lake Le Barge. In the driving snow, freezing wind, and darkness, they could hardly have picked a worse place. At their backs rose a wall of rock. Perrault and François had to make their fire and spread their sleeping robes on the ice of the lake itself. In order to travel light, they had gotten rid of their tent at Dyea.

Close in under the sheltering rock, Buck made his nest. It was so warm he hated to leave it when François handed out the fish. But when Buck finished eating and returned, he found his nest was occupied by Spitz. Outraged, he sprang at Spitz with a fury that surprised them both.

François was surprised, too, when they shot out of the nest. He saw the cause of the trouble. "Ah!" he cried to Buck. "Give it to him, the dirty thief!"

Spitz was crying with eagerness as he circled back and forth. Buck was no less eager, and no less cautious. But it was then that the unexpected happened.

The camp was suddenly alive with starving huskies, a huge pack of them. They must have smelled the camp from some Indian village. They had crept in while Buck and Spitz were fighting. When the two men sprang among them with their clubs, the huskies showed their teeth and fought back. They were crazed by the smell of food. They overturned the food box and scrambled for the bread and bacon. They yelped and howled under the blows of the clubs, but they struggled until the last crumb was gone.

In the meantime, the team dogs had burst out of their nests only to be set upon by the fierce invaders. Never had Buck seen such dogs. It seemed as though their bones would burst through their skins. But their hunger madness made them terrifying. The team dogs were swept back against the cliff. Buck was attacked by three huskies. His head and shoulders were soon ripped and slashed. Billee was crying as usual. Dave and Sol-leks, dripping blood from a dozen wounds, were fighting bravely side by side.

Perrault and François, having cleaned out their part of the camp, hurried to save their sled dogs. The wild wave of starving beasts rolled back before them, and Buck shook himself free. But it was only for a moment. The two men had to rush back to save what was left of their food. The huskies returned to the attack on the team. Billee, terrified into bravery, sprang through the savage circle and fled away over the ice. Pike and Dub followed on his heels, the rest of the team trailing behind.

Later, the nine team dogs gathered together and looked for shelter in the forest. There was not one who was not wounded in several places, some seriously. At daybreak they limped back to camp. The invaders were gone, and both men were in a bad temper. Half their food supply was gone. François looked over his wounded dogs.

"Ah, my friends," he said softly, "maybe it make you mad dog, those many bites. Maybe all mad dog, sacredam! What you think, eh, Perrault?"

The messenger shook his head. There

were still 400 miles of trail between here and Dawson. He could not afford to have madness break out among his dogs. It took two hours to get the harnesses in shape and get the team under way.

The next six days were filled with hardship and danger as they traveled up Thirty Mile River. There was a cold snap, and the temperature was 50 degrees below zero. But the river's wild water held off the frost. A dozen times Perrault fell through the ice near the edge. Each time this forced him to build a fire and dry his clothes.

Once, the sled broke through the ice along with Dave and Buck. They were half-frozen and all but drowned by the time they were dragged out. Again, a fire was necessary to save them because they were coated with ice. Then the two men ran them around the fire until they thawed out.

By the time they made the Hootalinqua and good ice, the dogs were played out. But Perrault, to make up for lost time, pushed them late and early. Buck's feet were not as hard as the feet of the huskies. All day long he limped in agony. Once camp was made, he lay down like a dead dog. François had to bring him his ration of fish. He rubbed Buck's feet for half an hour each night after supper. He also made Buck four little moccasins. Later, when Buck's feet grew hard on the trail, the worn-out moccasins were thrown away.

At the Pelly one morning, Dolly suddenly went mad and sprang straight for Buck. He had never seen a dog go mad. But he sensed that there was good reason to fear madness. Buck fled, with Dolly chasing right behind him, snarling. François, carrying an axe, called out to him. As Buck shot toward him, the axe crashed down upon mad Dolly's head.

Surprised, Buck staggered against the sled. This was Spitz's chance. He sprang upon Buck, sinking in his teeth and tearing his flesh to the bone. Then François got out his lash and gave Spitz a severe whipping.

"One devil, that Spitz," said Perrault. "Some day him kill that Buck."

"That Buck *two* devils," François replied. "All the time I watch that Buck I know for sure. Listen, some fine day him get mad like hell. Then

THE CALL OF THE WILD

him chew that Spitz all up and spit him out on the snow. Sure. I know."

From then on it was war between them. Spitz, as lead dog of the team, felt his rule threatened by this strange dog from the Southland. It was his pride that made him fear Buck as a possible rival for lead dog. And Buck, because of his own pride, was looking forward to the clash. He began to openly challenge Spitz's leadership.

One night there was a heavy snowfall. In the morning, Pike did not appear. He was hidden in his nest under a foot of snow. François couldn't find him. Spitz ran around the camp, snarling so loudly that Pike heard him in his hiding place. When Pike was discovered, Spitz flew at him to punish him. But Buck, with equal rage, jumped in between. So unexpected was the attack that Spitz was thrown backward in the snow. Pike, taking heart at this open mutiny, sprang upon Spitz. Buck did the same. But François saw what had happened and drove Buck off with his lash.

In the days that followed, as they got closer to Dawson, Buck continued to interfere between Spitz and other dogs. But he only did it when François was not around. Things no longer went smoothly with the dog team. There was constant trouble, and Buck was at the bottom of it.

After resting up in Dawson for seven days, they were back on the Yukon Trail. Now Perrault was carrying messages that were even more urgent than those he had brought in. He planned to make the trip to Dyea in record time. The snow on the trail was now packed hard. And because the police had arranged to leave food for them in several places, they were traveling light.

They made Sixty Mile in one day. But such good time had not been easy to achieve. The revolt led by Buck had destroyed the team spirit. No more was Spitz a leader to be feared. The dogs constantly fought. François's lash was always singing among the dogs, but it was of little use.

One night after supper, Dub came upon a snowshoe rabbit. But the quick rabbit got away, speeding down the frozen river. In a second the whole team was in full cry, chasing after the rabbit. Buck led the pack, his body streaking forward, leap by leap, in the moonlight.

Spitz left the pack and cut across a narrow neck of land where the river made a long bend. As the rabbit rounded the bend, Spitz leaped from the bank, his teeth breaking the rabbit's back in midair. When the rabbit shrieked in agony, Buck drove in on Spitz, shoulder to shoulder. They rolled over and over in the powdery snow. Then Spitz gained his feet, slashing Buck down the shoulder and leaping clear.

In a flash, Buck knew that the time had come. This time it would be to the death. They circled about, snarling, ears laid back. The other dogs drew up in a silent circle, their eyes gleaming. Spitz was a practiced fighter. Bitter rage was his—but never *blind* rage. He never rushed until he was prepared to receive a rush. He never attacked until he had first defended himself from attack.

In vain Buck tried to sink his teeth into the neck of the big white dog. Wherever his fangs struck for the softer flesh, they were met by Spitz's fangs. Fang clashed fang,

their lips cut and bleeding, but Buck could not get through his enemy's guard. Time and time again he tried for the snow-white throat. Yet each time, Spitz slashed back and got away.

Spitz was untouched, while Buck was streaming with blood and panting hard. The fight was growing desperate. And all the while the silent and wolfish circle waited patiently for their part in this drama—to finish off whichever dog went down.

Buck now showed a quality that made for greatness—imagination. He rushed in, but at the last instant, swept low to the snow and up. His teeth closed on Spitz's left foreleg. There was a crunch of breaking bone, and the white dog faced him on three legs. Buck then repeated the trick and broke the right foreleg. Despite the pain, Spitz tried to struggle on. He saw the silent circle closing in on him.

There was no hope for Spitz. Mercy was a thing for gentler climates. Making his final rush, Buck sprang in and brought Spitz down. The dark circle became a dot on the moonlit snow as Spitz disappeared from view. Buck stood and looked on. He was the champion—the wild beast who had made his kill and found it good.

| 6 |
Leader of the Pack

"Eh? What I say? I speak true when I say that Buck two devils."

This was François's speech the next morning when he discovered Spitz missing and Buck covered with wounds.

"That Spitz fight like hell," said Perrault as he looked over Buck's rips and cuts.

"And that Buck fight like *two* hells," François answered. "So now we make good time. No more Spitz, no more trouble."

While Perrault packed up and loaded the sled, François harnessed the dogs. Buck trotted up to the place Spitz would have taken as leader. But François, not noticing him, brought Sol-leks to this position. In his judgment, Sol-leks was the best lead dog left. Buck sprang upon Sol-leks in a fury, driving him back and taking his place.

"Eh? eh?" François cried. "Look at that Buck. Him kill that Spitz, him think he take the job."

"Go away!" he cried, but Buck stood fast and refused to move.

François dragged Buck to one side and put Sol-leks in place. The old dog did not like showing it, but he was afraid of Buck. When François turned his back, Buck again pushed Sol-leks from his place.

François became angry. "Now I fix you!" he cried, coming toward Buck with a heavy club in his hand.

Buck remembered the man in the red sweater. He stepped back, circling just beyond the range of the club, snarling with rage. François went about his work. He called to Buck when he was ready to put him in his old place in front of Dave. Buck retreated a few steps. When François followed after him, he retreated a few more steps. Then François threw down his club. He thought that Buck was afraid of a beating. But Buck was in open revolt. He had decided that leadership was his by right. Having earned it, he would not be happy with anything less.

François, with Perrault's help, ran Buck around for almost an hour. They threw clubs at him. He dodged. When they cursed him, Buck answered with a snarl, keeping out of their reach. He did not try to run away, but retreated around and around the camp. He made it clear that when they gave him what he wanted, he would be good.

François sat down and scratched his head. Perrault looked at his watch and swore. Time was flying. They should have been on the trail already. François looked at Perrault, who shrugged his shoulders to show that they were beaten. Then François put Sol-leks back in his old place. Now there was no place for Buck except at the front.

François called out, and Buck came to take his position at the head of the team. His traces were fastened. Soon they were off and running, out onto the river trail.

At once Buck took up the duties of leadership. He was quick thinking and quick acting where judgment was needed. He proved to be a better leader even than Spitz. Dave and Sol-leks did not mind the change in leadership. As long as they could do their work, they did not care what happened. But the rest of the team had grown unruly during Spitz's last days. They were in for a surprise as Buck began to lick them into shape.

Pike had never worked an ounce more than he had to. Now he was shaken again and again for loafing. Before the first day was done, he was pulling more than ever before in his life. The first night in camp, Buck punished Joe, the sour one—a thing that Spitz had never been able to do. Buck cut him up until he stopped snapping and began to whine for mercy.

The mood of the team picked up immediately. Once more the dogs leaped as one dog in the traces. At the Rink Rapids two huskies, Teek and Koona, were added to the team. Buck broke them in so quickly that it took François's breath away.

"Never such a dog as that Buck!" he cried. "No, never! Him worth one thousand dollars, eh? What you say, Perrault?"

Perrault nodded. He was very pleased with the team. They were making excellent time.

The Thirty Mile River was coated with ice. What had taken them ten days on the last trip they now covered in one day. They were averaging 40 miles a day. At the end of the 14th day they arrived at Skagway—in record time.

On their third day in Skagway, Perrault and François received official orders from the Canadian government. François called Buck to him. He threw his arms around the big dog and wept over him. That was the last Buck saw of François and Perrault. Like all the other men, they passed out of his life for good.

A Scotchman then took charge of Buck and his mates. In company with a dozen other dog teams, he started back over the weary trail to Dawson. This trip was not run in record time, for this was the mail train. They were carrying word from the world to the men who were seeking gold. It was a hard trip, with the big mailbags on board. The heavy work wore them down. They were in poor condition when they finally made Dawson.

The team should have had at least a week's rest in Dawson. But in two days they were back on the trail, loaded with letters for the outside.

The dogs were tired and the drivers grumbled. To make matters worse, it snowed every day. This meant a softer trail, and heavier pulling for the dogs. But the drivers treated them fairly and did their best for the weary animals.

Each night the dogs were fed before the drivers ate. And no man went to sleep before taking care of the dogs' feet. Still, the dogs were losing strength. Since the beginning of the winter they had traveled 1,800 miles. And they had dragged sleds the whole weary distance. Buck stood it, keeping his mates up to their work. But he, too, was very tired.

It was Dave who suffered most of all. Something had gone wrong with him. He became very moody. When he had to start pulling the sled, he would cry out in pain. One night the drivers brought him near the fire and examined him. But they couldn't seem to find out what was wrong with him.

By the time they reached Cassiar Bar, Dave was so weak that he kept falling in the traces. The Scotchman called a halt and took Dave out of the team. He wanted to give Dave a rest by letting him run free behind the sled. But Dave didn't like being taken out. His pride was hurt. He could not bear for another dog to do his work.

When the sled started, Dave refused to run quietly behind it. He kept trying to leap back inside the traces. Finally, weakened by this effort, he fell—and lay where he fell. The last his mates saw of him, Dave lay gasping in the snow. They could hear him howling sadly as they moved away.

Then the sled train was halted. The Scotchman walked slowly back to the camp. A gunshot rang out. The man came back in a hurry. The whips snapped, the bells tinkled, and the sleds sped along the trail. But Buck knew, and every dog knew, what had taken place back at the camp.

| 7 |
The Toil of
Trace and Trail

Thirty days after leaving Dawson, the Scotchman and his team arrived at Skagway. The dogs were dead tired, worn out and worn down. Buck's 140 pounds had dropped to 115. Sol-leks and Pike were limping. Dub was suffering from injuries to his shoulderblade.

The drivers had expected a long stay in Skagway. They felt entitled to a rest. But huge piles of mail were waiting for delivery in both directions. Then official orders arrived—sell the dogs and replace them with fresh ones.

On the fourth day, two men from the States came by. They bought the dog team, harness and all, for a song. Charles was a middle-aged man with watery eyes and a big mustache. Hal was around 19 or 20. He had a big Colt revolver and a hunting knife strapped on his belt. Both men seemed out of place in the Northland.

When Buck saw money exchange hands, he knew that the Scotchman was passing out of his life—just like Perrault and François and the others all had. Then his new owners brought the team to their camp. A woman, Mercedes, was there. She was Charles's wife and Hal's sister.

Buck watched as they took down their tent and loaded the sled. They rolled up their tent in a clumsy manner. Their tin dishes were packed away unwashed. Mercedes gave lots of advice about where to put things on the sled.

Three men from a nearby tent came out to watch. They were grinning and winking at one another.

"I wouldn't take that tent along if I was you," one of them said.

"How in the world could I manage without a tent?" cried Mercedes.

"It's springtime. You won't get any more cold weather," the man explained.

She shook her head. Charles and Hal

piled the last odds and ends on top of their huge load.

"It looks a bit top-heavy," said the man. "Do you think the dogs can run all day with that heavy load behind them?"

"Certainly," said Hal, taking hold of the gee-pole with one hand and swinging his whip with the other. "Mush!" he shouted. "Mush on there!"

The dogs sprang against their harness bands. For a few moments they strained hard, then stopped. They were unable to move the sled.

"The lazy brutes! I'll show them!" Hal cried angrily. He got ready to lash out at them with the whip.

But Mercedes cried, "Oh, no, Hal, you mustn't!" She caught hold of the whip and took it from him. "The poor dears! Now you must promise that you won't be harsh with them for the rest of the trip."

"A lot *you* know about dogs!" her brother sneered. "They're lazy, I tell you. You've got to whip them to get anything out of them. Just ask one of those men."

"The dogs are weak as water," came the reply from one of the men. "They need a rest."

"Never mind that man," Mercedes said to her brother. "*You're* driving our dogs. You do what you think is best with them."

Again Hal's whip fell upon the dogs. They pulled with all their strength. But the sled held as if it were anchored. Mercedes dropped to her knees before Buck. There were tears in her eyes as she put her arms around his neck.

"You poor, poor dears," she cried. "Why don't you pull harder? Then you won't have to be whipped."

The dogs inched forward. A hundred yards ahead the path turned and sloped steeply into the main street. As they swung on the turn, the sled went over, spilling half its load. The dogs never stopped. They were angry because of their ill treatment and the heavy load. Buck was raging. He broke into a run, the team following his lead. Hal cried, "Whoa! Whoa!" But they didn't listen. Then Hal tripped and was pulled off his feet. The sled ground over him, and the dogs dashed

ahead. The rest of the load was scattered along Skagway's main street.

Kind people on the street caught the dogs and gathered up the scattered belongings. They also gave advice: *Half the load and twice the dogs.* That is, if they ever expected to reach Dawson. Hal and Charles and Mercedes went through their belongings. They got rid of article after article. Mercedes cried over each thing that was thrown out.

Charles and Hal bought six outside dogs. These, added to the original six, plus Teek and

Koona, brought the team up to 14 dogs. But the outside dogs did not seem to know anything. Buck quickly taught them their places, and what not to do. But he could not teach them what *to* do. They did not take kindly to trace and trail.

Hal and Charles felt proud. They had never seen a sled with as many as 14 dogs. They felt that they were doing things in style. Of course, there was a *reason* why 14 dogs should not be used to pull a sled in the Arctic. One sled simply cannot carry enough food for 14 dogs. But Charles and Hal did not know this.

Late the next morning Buck led the team up the street. They were starting out dead weary. Having to face the long trail to Dawson again made Buck feel bitter. His heart was not in the work, nor was the heart of any dog. The outsider dogs were timid and frightened. The other dogs on the team had lost all confidence in their masters.

Buck felt that he could not depend upon these people. They did not know how to do anything. And it became clear that they would not learn. They did not know how to work the dogs. And they did not know how to work themselves.

It took them half the night to pitch camp, and half the morning to break the camp and load the sled. Some days they were unable to get started at all. When they did travel, they had to stop often to rearrange the load.

One day Hal noticed that his dog food was half gone, but they had only covered one quarter of their route. He decided to give the dogs less food and try to increase the day's travel. But the dogs needed rest even more than food. It was impossible to make the dogs travel faster in their weakened condition. Some of the dogs might not have enough strength to keep on going.

The first to go was Dub. His wrenched shoulderblade, untreated and unrested, went from bad to worse. Finally, Hal shot Dub with the big Colt revolver. It is said that an outside dog starves to death on the ration of the husky. So the six outside dogs, who were getting only *half* the ration the huskies normally got, died off one by one.

As in a nightmare, Buck staggered along at the head of the team. He pulled when he could. When he could no longer pull, he fell down. And he remained down until blows from a whip or club drove him to his feet again. Soon Buck and the other six remaining dogs looked like bags of bones.

There came a day when Billee fell and could not rise. Hal knocked Billee on the head with his axe, and dragged his body out of the harness. On the next day, Koona went. Only five remained: Joe, Pike, Sol-leks, Teek, and Buck, still at the head of the team.

It was beautiful spring weather, but neither dogs nor humans were aware of it. The days were growing longer. Under the blaze of sunshine, all things were thawing.

With the dogs falling, Mercedes weeping, Hal swearing, and Charles's eyes watering, they staggered into John Thornton's camp at the mouth of White River. When they halted, the dogs dropped as though they had all been struck dead at once.

Hal did the talking. John Thornton listened, and gave advice when it was asked.

Hal boasted about their luck at making it to White River, in spite of the melting ice. John Thornton said, "Only fools, with the blind luck of fools, could have made it. The bottom's likely to drop out at any moment. I tell you straight—I wouldn't risk my life on that ice for all the gold in Alaska."

"And that's because you're *not* a fool, I suppose," sneered Hal. "All the same, we'll go on to Dawson." He raised his whip. "Get up there, Buck! Mush on!"

But the team did not get up at his command. The whip flashed out, here and there. All the dogs except Buck slowly crawled to their feet. Buck made no effort. The lash bit him again and again. Watching, Thornton started to say something, but changed his mind. He got up and walked back and forth.

This was the first time Buck had failed. Hal, in a rage, exchanged his whip for the club. But Buck still refused to move. Like his mates, he was barely able to move. But unlike them, he had made up his mind *not* to get up. Buck had felt the thin and rotten ice under his feet all day. He seemed to sense disaster ahead, and so he refused to stir. No longer could he feel pain from the blows that continued to fall upon him. He felt numb all over. He was barely alive.

Suddenly, without any warning, John Thornton cried out and sprang upon the man with the club. Hal was hurled backward. Mercedes screamed. Charles watched but didn't get up.

John Thornton stood over Buck, trying to control himself. "If you strike that dog again, I'll kill you," he said.

"It's *my* dog," Hal said, wiping the blood from his mouth. "Get out of my way. I'm going to Dawson."

Thornton stood between Hal and Buck. Hal drew his long hunting knife. Mercedes was screaming. Thornton hit Hal's knuckles with the axe handle, knocking the knife to the ground. Then Thornton picked up the knife and cut Buck's traces.

Hal had no fight left in him. Besides, Buck was too near dead to be of further use in hauling the sled. A few minutes later the sled pulled away from the bank and down the river. Buck raised his head to watch. Pike was leading, followed by Sol-leks, Joe, and Teek. All four dogs were limping and staggering.

As Buck looked on, Thornton knelt beside

him and searched his body for broken bones. He found nothing more than many bruises and a state of starvation. By this time the sled was a quarter of a mile away. Dog and man watched it crawling along the ice.

Suddenly, they saw the sled's back end drop down, as into a rut. Then a whole section of ice gave way, and the dogs and humans disappeared! A hole in the ice was all that was to be seen. The bottom had dropped out of the trail.

"You poor devil," said John Thornton, and Buck licked his hand.

| 8 |
For the Love of a Man

John Thornton's feet had gotten frozen the previous December. His partners made him comfortable and left him to get well. They had headed up the river to get a raft of saw-logs to Dawson. At the time he rescued Buck, Thornton was still limping slightly. But with the continued warm weather, the limp finally left him. Now Thornton and Buck spent the long spring days lying by the riverbank. And here, watching the running water and listening to the songs of birds and the hum of nature, Buck won back his strength.

A rest is very welcome after one has traveled 3,000 miles. Buck grew lazy as his wounds healed. His muscles swelled out, and the flesh came back to cover his bones. They were all loafing—Buck, John Thornton, and his dogs, Skeet and Blackie. They were waiting for the raft that was to carry them down to Dawson.

Skeet was a little Irish setter who made friends with Buck early on. Just as a mother cat tenderly washes her kittens, so she washed and cleaned Buck's wounds. Blackie was a huge, good-natured black dog with eyes that laughed.

To Buck's surprise these dogs showed no jealousy toward him. They seemed to share John Thornton's kindness. As Buck grew stronger, he played all kinds of silly games with them. Buck was happy. And for the first time in his life he felt love. Back in California, he had experienced feelings of warm friendship toward Judge Miller. But it had taken John Thornton to arouse feelings of real love.

Not only had this man saved his life, but he was the ideal master. He took care of his dogs as if they were his children, not from a sense of duty. He had a way of taking Buck's

head between his hands, and resting his own head upon Buck's. He would shake the big dog back and forth, calling him names that Buck took for love names.

Buck went wild with happiness when Thornton touched him or spoke to him. He would lie for hours at Thornton's feet, studying each expression on the man's face. When they caught each other's gaze, the look in their eyes expressed their love for each other.

For a long time after his rescue, Buck did not like Thornton to get out of his sight. He would follow at the man's heels all day long. Buck was afraid that Thornton would pass out of his life as Perrault and François and the Scotchman had.

But despite his great love for Thornton, the wild instincts that the Northland had aroused in Buck remained alive. He was a thing of the wild—come in from the wild to sit by John Thornton's fire. Buck was no longer a dog of the soft Southland. He had learned well the harsh law of club and fang: *Kill or be killed; eat or be eaten.*

From the forest a mysterious call often sounded. Whenever Buck heard it, he was drawn to turn his back on the fire and plunge into the forest. But once inside the forest, his love for John Thornton drew him back to the fire again. Thornton alone held him. The rest of mankind was as nothing to Buck.

One day, Thornton's partners, Hans and Pete, arrived on the raft. Buck refused to notice them until he learned they were close to Thornton. After that he tolerated them.

Thornton, his partners, and the dogs traveled to Dawson on the raft. When they got there, they sold the raft and bought supplies. They then traveled to the head-waters of the Tanana. By then, Hans and Pete had become aware of Buck's amazing devotion to Thornton. One day Pete said, "I'd hate to be the man who lays hands on you when Buck's around."

Later that year, at Circle City, Pete's warning came true. A man called Burton had been picking a quarrel with another man at the bar. Thornton stepped between them. Buck was lying in a corner, watching his master's every action. Then, without warning, Burton struck out and sent Thornton spinning.

Those who were looking on heard neither bark nor yelp, but a roar. They saw Buck's body rise up in the air as he plunged for Burton's throat. The man saved his life by throwing out his arm. But he was slammed to the floor with Buck on top of him. And his throat was torn open. A doctor was able to stop the bleeding. The people decided that Buck had been provoked and let him go. From that day on, Buck's name spread through every mining camp in Alaska.

In the fall of that year, Buck saved Thornton's life in a different way. The three partners were trying to bring their narrow pole-boat down a bad stretch of rapids on Forty Mile Creek. At a certain bad spot, where a ledge of rock jutted out into the river, the boat turned over. Thornton, flung out of it, was carried downstream toward the worst part of the rapids. Ahead was a stretch of wild water in which no swimmer could survive.

In an instant Buck jumped into the mad swirl of water. When he felt Thornton grasp his tail, Buck headed for the bank, pulling with all his strength. Striking a rock, Thornton grabbed the slippery top with both hands, letting go of Buck. Above the water's roar, he yelled, "Go, Buck! *Go!*"

Sweeping downstream, Buck was finally able to fight his way to the bank. Pete and Hans tied a rope around his neck and shoulders. Then Buck jumped back into the water and swam toward Thornton. As Buck swept past him, Thornton reached out and threw both arms around the shaggy neck. Then Pete and Hans pulled them in toward the bank. Safely on shore, Thornton went over Buck's body and found three broken ribs.

"That settles it," said Thornton. "We camp right here 'til Buck is able to travel."

That winter, at Dawson, Buck became famous because of another incident. The three partners wanted to go to an area called the East, in search of a lost mine. But they didn't have the money to outfit themselves for such a trip.

Then, in the Eldorado Saloon, they got into a conversation. The other miners were boasting about their best dogs. One man said that his dog could start a sled with 500 pounds and walk off with it. A second said his dog could pull 600 pounds, and a third, 700.

John Thornton said, "Buck can start 1,000 pounds, break it out, and walk off with it for 100 yards."

A man named Matthewson said, "Ha! Well, I've got $1,000 that says he can't." He slammed down a small sack of gold dust upon the bar.

Nobody spoke. Thornton's bluff, if bluff it was, had been called. He didn't know if Buck could start 1,000 pounds—half a ton! Further, he did not have $1,000, nor did Hans or Pete.

"I've got a sled outside that's loaded with 20 50-pound sacks of flour," Matthewson went on.

"So don't let that stop you."

Thornton did not reply. He did not know what to say. Then he saw a familiar face in the crowd, his old friend Jim O'Brien.

"Can you lend me $1,000?" he asked, almost in a whisper.

"Sure," answered O'Brien. "But I've got little faith, John, that *any* beast can do such a trick."

Then Matthewson, sensing there was more easy money to be made, said, "Three to one for any other money you'd care to bet. What do you say?"

Thornton, Hans, and Pete could come up with only another $200 between them. They laid it down against Matthewson's $600.

The crowd in the Eldorado flowed out into the street. Several hundred men stood around Matthewson's sled. Loaded with 1,000 pounds of flour, the sled had been standing for a couple of hours. In the 60 degrees below zero cold, its runners had frozen fast to the hard-packed snow.

The team of 10 dogs was unhitched. Buck, with his own harness, was put in their place. He had caught the excitement. In some way he knew that he must now do a great thing for John Thornton.

The crowd grew silent as Thornton knelt by Buck's side. He took his head between both hands and rested cheek on cheek. He whispered in Buck's ear, *"As you love me, Buck."* Buck whined with eagerness.

Then Thornton stepped back and said, "NOW, Buck!"

Buck tightened the traces, then let them out for several inches. It was the way he had learned.

"GEE!" Thornton's voice rang out.

Buck swung to the right and then stopped with a sudden jerk. The load shook.

"HAW!" Thornton shouted.

Buck made the same move, but to the left. The sled's runners slipped several inches to the side. The sled was broken out! The men in the crowd were holding their breath.

"Now, MUSH!"

Thornton's command cracked out like a pistol shot. Buck threw himself forward, tightening the traces. His great chest was low to the ground, his head forward and down. All his muscles were straining. His feet were flying like mad, his claws making grooves in the hard-packed snow.

The sled swayed. Then it moved forward, ever so slowly, in a series of jerks—half an inch . . . an inch . . . two inches. Gradually it gained speed and moved steadily along.

Men gasped and began to breathe again. Thornton was running behind, cheering Buck on. Soon Buck passed the pile of firewood that marked the end of the 100 yards. He halted on command. Cheers grew into a roar. Hats and mittens flew into the air. Even Matthewson was cheering. Men were shaking hands; it did not matter with whom.

Thornton fell on his knees beside Buck and hugged him. Thornton's eyes were wet, and tears were streaming down his cheeks.

| 9 |

The Sounding
of the Call

In five minutes Buck had earned $1,600 for John Thornton. That made it possible for his master and his partners to journey into the East. Many had already gone in search of the lost gold mine, but few had returned. Those who did brought back nuggets of gold that were unlike any other gold in the Northland.

Months of searching went by. They sledded 70 miles up the Yukon. Then they followed the Stewart River until it became a narrow stream. At the end of all their wandering, they found not the lost gold mine, but a rich deposit of gold down at the bottom of the river valley. The three men searched no farther. Each day they worked earned them thousands of dollars in gold dust and nuggets. They stored the gold in moosehide bags, each bag holding 50 pounds.

There was nothing for the dogs to do, except haul in meat that Thornton had hunted now and then. Buck often grew restless. Something was calling him, but he did not know what it was. He would be lying in camp, dozing lazily. Then his head would suddenly lift and his ears cock up. He would spring to his feet and dash away into the forest. He would then spend hours exploring the hidden corners of the forest. Always Buck was seeking the mysterious something that called. It called, waking or sleeping, at all times, for him to come.

One night he sprang from sleep with a start. From the forest came the familiar call—a long-drawn howl. It was the same sound Buck had heard before. He ran through the sleeping camp and dashed into the woods in the direction of the cry. When Buck came to an open place among the trees, he stopped short. There he saw, sitting tall with its nose pointed to the sky, a long, lean timber wolf.

Buck had made no noise, but the wolf fled at sight of him. Buck followed, leaping through the woods. Finally, he caught up with the wolf and cornered him in a creek bed. The wolf snarled and snapped. Buck did not attack, but circled around him. The wolf was afraid. Buck weighed three times as much and the wolf's head barely reached Buck's shoulder. As soon as he had a chance, the wolf ran away and the chase continued.

Buck felt wild happiness. At last he was answering the wild and mysterious call. He was running by the side of his wood brother toward the place from where the call surely came.

When they stopped by a running stream to drink, Buck remembered John Thornton. After a moment, he slowly started back the way they had come. The wild brother ran by his side, whining softly. Then the wolf sat down, pointed his nose upward, and howled. It was a sad howl. As Buck kept on his way, he heard it growing fainter until it was lost in the distance.

John Thornton was eating dinner when Buck dashed into camp. Springing upon Thornton, he felt great joy at seeing him again. For two days and nights Buck never left camp. But then the call in the forest began to sound again, stronger than ever. Buck became restless. Once again he roamed through the woods in search of his wild brother. He began to sleep out at night, staying away from camp for days at a time.

Whenever Buck left the camp, he became a thing of the wild. He became an expert hunter who killed to eat. His usual prey included small animals, birds, and fish.

One day he was starting back toward camp and John Thornton. But as he got closer, he sensed that something was wrong. Soon he came upon Blackie. The huge dog was lying on his side, dead. An arrow was sticking out of his body.

Then the faint sound of many voices, rising and falling in a singsong chant, came from the camp. Creeping forward to the edge of the clearing, Buck found Hans. He was lying on his face. The many arrows in his back made him look like a porcupine.

At that instant, Buck looked toward the center of their camp. What he saw filled him with rage. Because of his great love for John Thornton, he lost his head.

Yeehat Indians were dancing about the ruins of the camp! Buck hurled himself at them in a frenzy to destroy. First he sprang at the chief of the Yeehats, ripping his throat wide open. Not stopping for an instant, he leaped at a second man, tearing wide his throat. So rapid were Buck's movements that the Indians were shooting one another with their arrows. Then, in a wild panic, the Yeehats fled screaming into the woods.

Buck raged at their heels, dragging them down like deer as they raced through the trees.

The Yeehats scattered far and wide over the country. It was not until a week later that the last of the survivors gathered together and counted their losses.

Buck returned to the ruined camp. He found Pete where he had been killed in his blankets at the first moment of surprise. At the edge of a deep pool lay Skeet, faithful to the last. And in the pool, Buck found the body of John Thornton.

All day Buck stayed by the pool or roamed around the camp. He knew that John Thornton was dead. This gave Buck a cold, empty feeling inside—an emptiness that food could not fill.

Night came on, and a full moon rose high over the trees. Buck stood up, listening. From far away came a faint, sharp yelp, followed by a chorus of yelps. It was the call, sounding more appealing now than ever before. And as never before, he was ready to obey. John Thornton was dead. The last tie was broken. Man and the claims of man no longer bound him.

Hunting their prey, the wolf pack had at

last invaded Buck's valley. Into the moonlit clearing they came in a silvery flood. In the center of the clearing stood Buck, as still as a statue, waiting for them. The boldest wolf leaped straight at him. Like a flash Buck struck, breaking its neck. Three others tried. One after the other they drew back, blood streaming from their wounds.

Then the whole pack attacked, eager to pull down the prey. But Buck was so quick, he seemed to be everywhere at once. Whirling and leaping from side to side, Buck kept snapping and gashing. At the end of half an hour the wolves drew back. Their tongues were hanging out, and their fangs shone white in the moonlight.

One wolf came up to Buck in a friendly manner. Buck recognized the wild brother with whom he had run for a night and a day. He was whining softly. As Buck whined in answer, they touched noses. Then the rest of the pack came forward. Buck sniffed noses with them, too. Then the entire wolf pack sat down and began to howl.

Now the call came to Buck. He, too, sat

down and howled. After a few minutes, the pack crowded around him, sniffing in a half-friendly, half-savage manner. Then the pack sprang away into the woods, yelping in chorus. And this time Buck ran along with them, side by side with his wild brothers, yelping as he ran.

The Yeehats tell of a Ghost Dog that runs at the head of the wolf pack. They are afraid of this Ghost Dog. It steals from their camps and traps, kills their dogs, and is unafraid of their bravest hunters. Some of the best hunters fail to return to the camp. They are found with their throats slashed. In the snow the Yeehats see wolf prints that are larger than the prints of any wolf.

Each fall, when the Yeehats follow the moose, there is a certain valley they never enter. In the summer, there is one visitor to the valley. It is a great wolf, like—and yet unlike—all other wolves. He comes down into an open space among the trees. The Yeehats say that he sits there for a while. Before he leaves, he howls but once, long and sadly.

He is not always alone. When the long

winter nights come on, the Yeehats have seen the Ghost Dog in the pale moonlight, running at the head of the pack. Leaping gigantic above the other wolves, he can be heard singing the song of his world, which was the song of the pack.

Activities
The Call of the Wild

BOOK SEQUENCE
First complete the sentences with words from the box. Then number the events to show which happened first, second, and so on.

sniffed	knuckles	library	allow
howled	recognized	feet	wept
stranger	bartender	lifeless	mush

_____ 1. Francois threw his arms around Buck and _____ over him.

_____ 2. Buck lay at Judge Miller's feet by the fire in the _____.

_____ 3. Thornton hit Hal's _____ with the axe-handle.

_____ 4. Buck _____ at the white stuff he saw falling through the air.

_____ 5. Buck decided that he would never _____ another rope to be put around his neck.

_____ 6. Money passed between Manuel and a _____.

_____ 7. At last, Buck sat down with the pack and _____.

_____ 8. Perrault _____ that Buck was one in a thousand.

_____ 9. Buck learned to stop at "ho" and go ahead at "_____."

_____ 10. Every night, Francois rubbed Buck's sore _____ for half an hour.

_____ 11. Curly lay in the snow, limp and _____.

_____ 12. The ugly face of the _____ peeked in at Buck.

81

FACTS ABOUT CHARACTERS
Reread Chapter 1 and answer below.

A. Write the characters name from the box to complete sentences.

Santa Clara	Shep	Alice
San Diego	Mollie	Manuel

1. Trouble was coming for every strong dog from Puget Sound to _____.

2. _____ had a terrible weakness—he loved to gamble.

3. The Judge's daughters _____ and _____ would take Buck with them on early morning walks.

4. Buck's mother, _____, was a Scotch shepherd.

5. Judge Miller's place was in the sunny _____ valley.

B. Write **T** if the statement is *true* or **F** if the statement is *false*.

1. ___ Big dogs were needed in the frozen Southland.

2. ___ Gold had been discovered in the Klondike.

3. ___ Judge Miller's place was called College Park.

4. ___ The stranger threw Buck over on his back.

5. ___ Money was passed between Alice and Manuel.

COMPREHENSION CHECK

Reread Chapter 4 and answer below.

A. Circle a letter to correctly complete each sentence.

1. Buck's first day in the Northland was spent
   in a place called
   a. Miller's estate.
   b. Dyea Beach.
   c. Seattle.

2. The dogs and men Buck met there were
   a. savages.   b. civilized.   c. French-Canadian.

3. Buck learned that the "wolf manner of fighting"
   was to
   a. attack from the rear.
   b. punch with paws.
   c. strike and leap away.

4. To make sure the dogs obeyed him,
   Francois used a
   a. stern voice.   b. hatchet.   c. whip.

5. What did Buck watch another dog steal?
   a. bacon   b. salmon   c. bread

B. Explain each answer in your own words.

1. On his first night in camp, Buck couldn't find
   the other dogs. Where were they?
   They were _____

   _____

2. How were Dave and Sol-leks different on the
   trail than they were in camp?
   They were _____

   _____

CAUSE AND EFFECT

Reread Chapter 7 and write a letter in the blank to match each *cause* on the left with its *effect* on the right.

CAUSE

1. ____ The dogs get one-half of their food ration.

2. ____ To make them pull harder, Hal whips the dog team.

3. ____ The coming of spring brings blazing sunshine.

4. ____ Hal refuses Thornton's advice.

5. ____ Buck senses that disaster is just ahead.

6. ____ The outside dogs are too inexperienced to go out on the trail.

7. ____ The townspeople in Skagway suggest "half the load and twice the dogs."

8. ____ The dog team dashes down the steep slope into town.

9. ____ After too little rest, it takes the dogs 30 days to reach Skagway.

10. ____ Hal and Charles overload the sled.

EFFECT

a. They feel timid and frightened.

b. Hal's sled sinks beneath the melting ice.

c. The sled topples over, spilling its load.

d. He refuses to get up.

e. The dogs lose weight and suffer injuries.

f. The dogs become angry at their ill treatment.

g. The outside dogs die off, one by one.

h. Snow and ice begin to melt.

i. Hal is tripped and pulled off his feet.

j. Mercedes throws out many belongings.

IDIOMS

Reread Chapter 8. Then read the **boldfaced** idioms and circle a letter to show its meaning.

1. "I'd hate to be the man who **lays hands on** Thornton when Buck's around."

   a. pats or hugs

   b. grabs or hits

   c. tries to heal

2. Burton had been **picking a quarrel** with another man at the bar.

   a. starting a fight

   b. selecting a topic

   c. hitting with a pick

3. Thornton's bluff, if bluff it was, **had been called**.

   a. insults had been exchanged

   b. proof had been demanded

   c. charges had been made

4. From that day on, Buck's name **spread through** every mining camp in Alaska.

   a. flowed like water

   b. was printed on posters

   c. was widely mentioned

5. Matthewson sensed that there was **more easy money to be made**.

   a. coins to be counterfeited

   b. good pay for simple work

   c. more bets to be won

6. The crowd from the Eldorado **flowed out** into the street.

   a. came out all at once

   b. was caught in a flood

   c. came one at a time, like drops of water

FINAL EXAM

Circle a letter to correctly answer each question or complete each statement.

1. When the story begins in 1897, how old is Buck?

   a. two years old

   b. four years old

   c. about six months old

   d six years old

2. Why did Buck accept the rope from Manuel?

   a. He was often leashed this way.

   b. He thought it was a game.

   c. He trusted people he knew.

   d He liked to be roped.

3. Why did the stranger say he was taking Buck to San Francisco?

   a. to see a dog doctor

   b. to be in a dog show

   c. to see Judge Miller

   d to live in the city

4. From San Francisco, Buck was next taken by train to
   a. Skagway.
   b. the Klondike.
   c. College Park station.
   d Seattle.

5. Who called Buck a "red-eyed devil"?
   a. the Judge's sons
   b. Francois
   c. the man in the red sweater
   d the man in the baggage car

6. From the man in the red sweater Perrault bought
   a. Buck and Curly.
   b. Buck and Spitz
   c. Dave and Spitz
   d two fox terriers.

Answers to Activities
The Call of the Wild

BOOK SEQUENCE
1. 10/wept   2. 1/library   3. 11/knuckles   4. 6/sniffed
5. 4/allow   6. 2/stranger   7. 12/howled
8. 5/recognized   9. 8/mush   10. 9/feet
11. 7/lifeless   12. 3/bartender

FACTS ABOUT CHARACTERS
A. 1. San Diego   2. Manuel   3. Alice, Mollie
   4. Shep   5. Santa Clara
B. 1. F   2. T   3. F   4. T   5. F

COMPREHENSION CHECK
A. 1. b   2. a   3. c   4. c   5. a
B. 1. under the snow in their snow nests.
   2. much more alert and active.

CAUSE AND EFFECT
1. g   2. f   3. h   4. b   5. d   6. a   7. j   8. i   9. e   10. c

IDIOMS
1. b   2. a   3. b   4. c   5. c   6. a

FINAL EXAM: 1. b   2. c   3. a   4. d   5. c.   6. a